CUMBRIA LIBRARIES

3 8003 05176 2409

KT-151-715

The Littlest Bandit

To Grandmas and
Grandpas everywhere

SIMON & SCHUSTER

First published in Great Britain in 2020 by
Simon & Schuster UK Ltd
1st Floor, 222 Gray's Inn Road, London WC1X 8HB
A CBS Company

Text & illustrations copyright © Ali Pye 2020

The right of Ali Pye to be identified as the
author and illustrator of this work has been asserted by her in
accordance with the Copyright, Designs and Patents Act, 1988

All rights reserved, including the right of reproduction in whole or in part in any form

A CIP catalogue record for this book is available from the British Library upon request

HB ISBN: 978-1-4711-7252-6 ▪ PB ISBN: 978-1-4711-7253-3 ▪ eBook ISBN: 978-1-4711-7254-0
Printed in China   10 9 8 7 6 5 4 3 2 1

The Littlest Bandit

Ali Pye

SIMON & SCHUSTER

London   New York   Sydney   Toronto   New Delhi

The Littlest Bandit had been reading,
as usual, when Grandma Bandit

whizzed

overhead and landed in a tree.

Grandma had been trying to fly.

(Like most of the Bandit family, Grandma was something of a daredevil.)

"Are you alright, Grandma?" squeaked the Littlest Bandit, putting down her book.

"Totally fine, dear!" called Grandma from high up in the branches (it was a VERY tall tree). "I'm a tiny bit stuck though. Go and get some help, Littlest."

"I could help you," said the Littlest Bandit.

"Littlest Bandit, you have your nose
in a book all day!" smiled Grandma.
"I need some proper bandit skills.
Off you trot and fetch the family."

Soon the whole Bandit clan had gathered beneath the tree. They were a daring bunch and everyone had an idea about how to rescue Grandma.

"I can help," said the Littlest Bandit.
But nobody listened, as usual.

"Step aside, Littlest," said Uncle Bob Bandit,
who'd won medals for climbing.

"I'll be up that tree in a jiffy and
straight back down with Grandma."

But –
oh dear.

The tree was
so slippery that
Uncle Bob really did
come straight back down.

Just not with Grandma.

BUMPETY-BUMP!

Hmm, rescuing Grandma might be harder than expected.

"I can help!" said the Littlest Bandit,
a tiny bit louder.

But nobody noticed, as usual.

Auntie Sue Bandit pushed forward –
she was a world-champion gnawer.

"Hold on tight, Grandma!" she called.
"I'll bring that tree down with you in it."

It sounded dangerous.
Grandma looked excited.

But – oh no.

The tree was too
tough to gnaw and
Auntie Sue broke a tooth.

OUCH!

Even Grandma looked a bit worried now.
The bandits scratched their heads.

And then Grandma started to look REALLY worried . . .

An enormous, hungry-looking
eagle was flying straight
towards Grandma!

"Er… it might be time to get me down," she called,
"not that I'm scared of course, but . . .

YOU MIGHT WANT
TO HURRY!"

"I can help!!!" cried the Littlest Bandit, jumping up and down and waving her book around wildly.

But Grandpa Bandit pushed past her.

OOF!

"Back away!" shouted Grandpa.
"This calls for **extreme bandit skills**!

I'll see off that bird **AND** rescue you, Grandma."

OOOHHHH!

gasped the Bandits as Grandpa flew
through the air in a breathtaking stunt.

But – oh my goodness!
   The tree was too high and
      Grandpa landed in a pond.

Everyone was drenched, even the eagle.

The soggy bird flapped away –
but Grandma was still stuck in the tree.

No one knew what to do.

"I CAN HELP!"
yelled the Littlest Bandit.

**"IT'S ALL HERE IN
THIS BOOK!!!"**

"A book?" said the bandits. "How can a book help Grandma? She's stuck in a tree, if you haven't noticed."

"Just wait and see," said the Littlest Bandit. "I **am** a bandit, after all."

The family looked doubtful.

"She's right, you know," called Grandma from up high. "You have a go, Littlest. It's getting chilly and I want my tea!"

The Littlest Bandit took a deep breath and opened her book . . .

The family soon set to work, with
Littlest Bandit calling out instructions.

"Over here, Auntie Sue," she said,
and, "Left a bit, Uncle Bob."

"Get moving, everyone!" said Grandma.
"I've no idea what she's up to – but you
do what Littlest tells you."

And so they did. Until . . .

TA-DA!!!

With a hop, jump and a
skip, the Littlest Bandit
scampered up, up,
UP the pyramid . . .

and back down again

with Grandma.

"Wonderful!" said Grandma when they reached the ground.

"I haven't had so much fun in ages . . . shall we do it all again tomorrow?"

That night, the Bandit family had a big
noisy party. Grandma made a special cake
and the Littlest Bandit even put her book
down to eat it.

"Thank you for rescuing Grandma, Littlest," everyone said.

"You're welcome," smiled the Littlest Bandit, as she gave them all presents to read.

And after that, there was no stopping them.

It's AMAZING what you can find in a book!